AF278792

Princess

by

Martha Pendley

authorHOUSE®

AuthorHouse™
1663 Liberty Drive, Suite 200
Bloomington, IN 47403
www.authorhouse.com
Phone: 1-800-839-8640

First published by AuthorHouse   6/25/2008

ISBN: 978-1-4343-2278-4 (sc)

Printed in the United States of America
Bloomington, Indiana

This book is printed on acid-free paper.

In every life there is a story worth telling, but

too often the truth is buried deep in the past.

The West was changing.

By 1854, small bands of Navajo Indians had tired of fighting the never-ending hordes of white men. They simply moved over and built their villages of hogans and hide shelters in the semi-barren region of the eastern New Mexico Territory. They hunted and farmed where the foothills met the plains, plying their artistic skills on the simple elements of a peaceful existence, venturing short distances into the plains to herd sheep and a few cattle.

The Apache had ceased fighting the Navajo and turned to the White man who was a more worthy opponent for his warlike nature.

In Utah, the Mormons had spent seven years establishing and strengthening their hold in the Great Salt Lake Valley. Their missionaries rode through the Southwest spreading the gospel, making converts and taking wives.

What then did the Mormon have to do with the Navajo?

The Indian girl ran down the bluff and through the trees to the sandy flat where the big gray horse stood nosing the fallen man. She had watched them drink from the shallow river, had seen the horse buck and kick when the man tried to remount. She knew she should run, but she was strangely drawn. When she rolled him over, his eyes opened. Green eyes, as pale as the young willow leaves near the river, but crystal clear like shiny stones in the hill streams, and his hair was the deep red of the clay her tribe used to make pots!

He sat up and shook his head, stunned but not visibly hurt except for the ugly gash on his temple and the strangely twisted leg. She had seen white men from afar, but her tribe had been able to avoid contact, their meager existence offering little the white man wanted. This one needed help and he was in no condition to be a threat.

"Hello, Indian Princess, I must be dreaming!"

Anya shyly tugged at his arm to help him stand, and after a struggle he was able to balance himself on his good leg. The effort exhausted him, and pale and shaking, he slumped against his horse. The frightened girl again resisted the urge to run, but she knew he could not mount alone. After several painful failures, they got him in the saddle but he seemed too weak to sit upright. She bounded agilely up in front of him, pulled his arms around her body and walked the horse down the river to the small group of hogans. She had no fear for his safety. Her tribe was peaceful now, in spite of the dreadful tales they told around the fire at night. When she slipped from the saddle, the man fell also. Two strong women hurried to help him to a shelter made of hides stretched over poles, and others put aside their weaving to make room for the injured man.

She tethered the beautiful animal. Such a shame to burden it with the heavy saddle and pack. Later she would take them off, but now she rushed to help the women tend to her prize.

When he regained consciousness, his leg was bound in a bale of hide strips, and he had been placed on a mat under the shelter. Jon was a strong outdoor man, and the broken leg was only a nuisance to be endured, but the lump on his head from the horse's random kick was another matter. He was too dizzy to stand, and had no choice but to delay the important mission for his church and accept the unconcerned hospitality of the Indians.

The days passed slowly for the recuperating Mormon, and he marveled at the contented existence of his hosts. The women talked little, moving slowly with a studied grace, performing their simple tasks. The men were away from the village most of the day while the women combed and dyed wool, weaving it into colorful blankets and preparing meals in primitive fashion using handmade utensils. Only at night around the fire did the men become animated and vocal, using hand and body motions to better communicate. Through all this Jon was a spectator, not quite ignored, just passively accepted.

Gradually the swelling left his head and with it the dizziness and he was able to stand upright. The girl brought him a forked stick and he found he could hobble a few steps with the cumbersome wrapped leg dangling. Apparently she had been assigned to attend him, for she was always in sight ready to help him when he fell. The long hours of solitude tried the patience of the active man, and he longed for some kind of intellectual stimulation, but she was his only contact, and language was a problem. She seemed to enjoy the silence and resisted his efforts, but time was in his favor. Slowly they learned to converse, one word sentences, questioning looks, gestures, until laughingly they could name the objects and activities in the village in both tongues. Feelings, ideas, impressions were more difficult, but even these improved over the weeks as he learned to adopt her hand and body movements to express himself. He read aloud from a book he carried, and although she did not understand it, the sounds were pleasing and she was fascinated by the symbols. Her own language was oral, and could only be recorded by the pictures she drew for him in the sand. The bond grew stronger daily. With time on their hands, the pair slowly improved their communication skills. He was able to tell her about his wives and children in Utah. Anya tried to explain her position in the tribe. She and her mother lived on the edge of the village, taking part in all of the work of the tribe. They helped with the planting and harvesting, the hunting and fishing, weaving and pottery making, preparation of food and eating, but they withdrew when social activities arose. When Anya was small she played with the other children and they called her "Little Doe," but she grew taller and thinner and her long face and sharp features were so different, they avoided her and called her "Pache." The young men shunned her also, but noting her agility and her hunting skills with envy, they let her hunt with them, since she greatly outhunted them, and the game was shared.

His first trip to the river took all his strength. He had slipped away early one morning before she came out of her hogan. Sitting on the bank he struggled out of his clothes and dipped them in the clear water. They needed a wash as badly as he did. Drat that crazy horse, he should never have bought him; he had been warned. The trader's last words had been, "Good luck pal, I've taken my last tumble off old Jericho! He's all yours."

The thud of a running horse shook the ground and his gray galloped into view. The rider was not visible low on the horse's neck until her dark flying hair gave her away. He knew he could not reach the runaway in time, and the girl would be hurt! But she dropped easily to the ground before the horse stopped, and stripping off her loose garment, slid into the water. He watched in wonder at the sheer beauty of her, fluid as the water itself. Then he slipped down the bank.

From that time, the days were idyllic. The others in the village were unaware or uncaring that they spent their days together riding the horse, swimming and talking. He told her about the mountains so high they reached above the clouds, and about the sea where water lapped at white sands all day, about the river so wide it had to be crossed on a barge, and about his wives and children in Utah. She listened to the beloved voice but much he said was confusing to her.

When the day came that he was well enough to travel, he tried to explain to her that he had work to do for his God. She looked at his grim face, so unlike the one she had grown to love. "Your God make you not happy." She raised her arms in a wide arc. "My God good, give this, say be happy!" Holding her close he nearly gave in. Over the months he had changed so much. The teachings of his youth, the fiery lessons he himself had brandished for years, were foreign to him now. Those simple words spoken by the serene Indian girl seemed to penetrate his whole being, opening his eyes to the truth he had thought he was seeking. All his life he had been driven, first by his father and the leaders of the church, later by his own determination. Climb higher, fight harder! But now he had lost the urge to reach those goals. The meaning of life seemed so much simpler. He could not walk away from the Indian girl and from the deep contentment he had found. She would not fit in his old life, and he now knew he too would never belong there again. Surely there was just one God, and as he absorbed the nature of her belief, Jon felt the painful shattering of a lifetime of misplaced faith. Strangely, he felt free, at peace, and closer to God than he had ever believed possible.

"Princess, I have to leave you for a while, but I'll come back and be with you always. We will climb the beautiful mountains so tall they touch the clouds, and watch waves ripple on white sand, and you'll never have to share me with anyone. But to earn this happiness I have to keep one last promise." But still he lingered, unable to break the spell.

Several weeks later a train of freight wagons camped down the river and Jon bargained with them to take him to Fort Worth. It bothered them not at all that he was a Mormon living with the Indians. The ore they carried had been taken by white men from mines stolen from Indians. They were going to trade it for tools, food staples and household goods for themselves, and questionable items to appease the Indians. The answer to this West was survival, not loyalties.

Just at sunup they rode Jericho to the edge of the camp. "Princess, I will just be gone for a little while. I am going to fix things for us. I'll be back in six months, six full moons, before the first snow, and I'll take you with me then. We'll go East, across the wide river, and on to the sea. Just you and me, Princess. Look to the rising sun each day. I'll come back that way."

He left his book, with a mark for each day he would be gone, and showed her how to cross off the days with a soft rock. Anya took off her beads and offered them to him, but he put them back around her neck, stroking her dark head and kissing her again. "Always wear them so I will know my princess."

She missed Jon, but she had faith in his promise to return to her. She spent many hours now reminiscing about their months together, and her life before he came.

She and her mother had always lived on the fringe of the village, with it but not really a part of it. Her mother's family did not accept Anya, thus alienating her mother also. She remembered as a child they chided her and called her "Pache." Her mother seemed to withdraw further and draw her closer as she grew older. She realized she was somehow different. Her reflection in the clear pools was a slimmer face, more prominently featured than her flat-faced relatives. She wanted to ask her mother, but the sad-eyed woman seemed to pine away, until during the last snow, she had just gone to sleep forever. After her mother died, Anya lived alone on the edge of the village, working with them, but shunning offers of closer friendship.

And then Jon had come, filling her heart with happiness to make up for all her lonely years.

While she waited for Jon to return, she rode Jericho daily. He was as docile now as an Indian pony without the heavy saddle, and she kept Jon's book in a pocket of the blanket she threw over his back. Through the hot summer she marked off the days, but it was taking too long. Her waist was thickening. She watched the women of her tribe and she knew she would soon have to leave. If they knew, they would kill Jon when he returned and she would live in loneliness like her mother. She had to find him first.

Her people were preparing to move nearer the foothills to find grass for the herd. She slipped away on Jericho, taking nothing to arouse suspicion. She rode East, into the rising sun, where Jon had told her he would be. Food was no problem. She carried the dried meat, nuts and grain her people ate when they herded for weeks on the plain. Water was sometimes scarce, but the horse seemed to smell it and lead her to streams.

Her world was so small, she had no idea how far she would travel to find "east" but she was certain she could find Jon. For several weeks she rode at night when it was cool, stopping at dawn to sleep during the day in shaded places. She was careful to note the direction of the sun before she slept. Jericho never left her side, sensing her dependence on him. If animals or people came too near he nickered softly to waken her, but seldom was there cause for alarm. Sometimes she came upon small bands of Indians who welcomed her. By gesture and sign she made her position known. She was going into the rising sun to find the father of her baby. They let her rest and sent her on with food.

She passed white women and children working in the fields who sometimes bade her rest and take food. She avoided settlements and groups of men and several times she had to avoid large herds of cattle on the move. Only once did she and Jericho receive mistreatment. She surprised a group of boys fishing in a creek and they threw rocks and screamed "Squaw, squaw!" On warm nights she sometimes led Jericho and walked to stretch her tired limbs. But after many weeks the nights were too cool and she lay low on the horse to feel his warmth as she rode.

One day, just before sundown, they reached a river she could hardly see across. To her childlike mind this was a sign of hope, and she walked two days up the river until they found a river barge. The bargeman tried to explain that she had to pay to cross, but she did not understand. He touched her beads. "I'll take you and that elephant across for them beads." Anya backed away and shook her head, tears of exhaustion falling down her cheeks.

"Okay, kid, stay back in the trees. I'll take you and the big fellow across after dark, but stay out of sight. Can't have folks telling my wife I talked to an Indian, she'd throw me out."

After they crossed the big river, she lost heart. She had traveled so far and she was so tired. They found shelter in the woods at night now, and rode in the sun to keep warm. Drenching rains fell for a week, and the temperature dropped. They spent three days in a cave to escape thunderstorms. She had not even tried to find food for days. And she knew she was too weak to wait any longer. She could not mount the big horse, so she stumbled beside him to the settlement. At the first house with a light, she climbed the step and pounded on the door. When a man opened the door, she pointed to the horse, murmured "Jericho" and handing him her blanket and a book, she fell at his feet.

Jeremiah lifted the slight form and placed her on the hearth rug. He brought her broth from the stove and helped her drink it. "Jon's book" were the only words she uttered, and clasping it she closed her eyes. He watered the horse and pulled hay from the loft. An hour later, bone weary but triumphant, he held the beautiful baby, creamy skin, dark hair, certainly not all Indian. He awoke his eldest, Eliza, and she helped with the baby, but the mother never regained consciousness.

At dawn he picked up the book and read the name on the fly leaf, "Elder Jon Taylor, Church of Jesus Christ of the Latter Day Saints."

"My God, another abomination by the Mormons!" He tossed the book into the fire and watched it burn.

By the early morning light he carried the Indian woman to the knoll behind the house. He removed the colorful beads and put them in his coat pocket before he covered the grave. Then he divided the rain spattered flowers the children had placed on their mother's grave and placed some at the Indian girl's mound. It seemed fit. Now he realized the wisdom in burying his wife and stillborn baby together yesterday. The two new mounds would not be questioned.

Kneeling between the mounds, he read again the passages from his bible, and prayed, "The Lord giveth and the Lord taketh away. Blest be the name of the Lord. Amen."

When the weary man entered the house, the baby was asleep, mush was bubbling on the stove and Eliza had washed the Indian blanket and hung it on a chair by the fire to dry. "For the baby" she said. He nodded and took the beads from his pocket "For the baby." Jeremiah Phillips was profoundly grateful for his eldest daughter who, like her father had accepted the sadness and risen to the task at hand. His gentle pat on her shoulder said it all.

For several weeks they feared they would lose the baby. It was so small and weak. It only mewled softly, and slept day and night. But one morning, the entire family was awakened by a hearty cry and the baby sucked hungrily at the milk Elizabeth spooned into its tiny mouth. From that moment on the hardy Indian heritage took over and it grew and gained daily.

The children were happy with the new baby. Pa told them the events as he knew them, and made them take a vow on the Bible to keep the secret. "This baby is ours, it was sent to us. But folks won't take to an Indian if they know. Never let a breath of it outside this room."

Eliza who had seen the beautiful mother, insisted on an Indian name. "In her memory" she said tearfully, remembering her own mother so recently lost. They knew no Indian names except those of the notorious fighters, but brother Rass found the story in his school book about a friendly Indian girl named Pocahontas. The girls were thrilled. "We'll call her Pokey." The man reluctantly added Taylor. "She would want it that way." He said. So Pocahontas Taylor Phillips was her name.

In the early 1860's, war was ravaging the South, and tendrils of the conflict reached westward. A Yankee camp in Corinth, Mississippi, was creating havoc for the Phillips family and their neighbors. The small farms were stripped of all their resources to feed the soldiers.

Pokey was hanging on the gate post crying. She had helped Pa dig up the few turnip roots that had been overlooked by the greedy soldiers.

Her racking sobs distorted the sound of the approaching horse. It could have been her sisters breaking twigs to build a fire in the old stove, or cracking acorns to parch for coffee, or Pa still digging in last spring's garden for a last potato or turnip. It didn't matter.

Nothing. That was what they had. The smokehouse was empty. Last summer they dug up the dirt floor and soaked the salt out of the soil, but there was nothing left to salt now. All the jars of vegetables and fruit the girls had worked so hard to put up were gone too. The chickens, the cow. Only the old gray horse still stood in the lot, too old now to be of use to the soldiers. The mules. The Yankees would not know how to plow with them. When a horse snorted at her side, she lifted her tear-smudged face and stared at the man. He looked a little like her brother, Rass, who had gone to fight the Yankees . . two years ago now, or a lifetime to the seven-year old Pokey. She stopped sniveling and wiped her nose with the back of her dirty hand. She was ashamed of being caught. She never cried, not even when she fell off old Jericho, or when the children at school teased her and called her an Indian. But she was so hungry!

"Why are you crying, little sister?"

"I'm not your little sister! And you would cry too if you was hungry. The Yankees took our chickens, our cow and all of our food."

"Well now, that's bad. I've got a little sister at home like you."

The gentle voiced man rode off more noisily than he had come, leaving the puffy faced child to sit down and face the sad scene. Their home was on the edge of town, the rutted road really just a lane. The house had been pretty to Pokey before the Yankees came, but now it looked as bad as she felt. Most of the furniture was gone, the rockers off the porch, all the farm tools except the old broken handled hoe her father was using. They even took the good dishes and the pots. Two years of hunger and need were telling on even the happy child who lived in her own dream world, the mystery of her origin remaining her secret joy. She told herself variations of the tale about the night in the middle of the early fall rains when an Indian woman came to the door and asked to sleep on the hearth. In Corinth, Mississippi, 1855, Indians seldom came to town and when they did, they were avoided. But Pa said he couldn't turn her out in the storm. That night Pokey was born and her mother died, and the Indian begged to name the child, leaving her a beaded necklace and a blanket. So Pocahontas Taylor Phillips was born. When she asked Pa about the Taylor in her name, he said that was her mother's name. Sister Mary was Mary Ella, and Margaret was Margaret Ann. Eliza Beth was the oldest. Pokey liked their names, but she was proud to have her mother's name for her second one, in spite of, or because of the mystery surrounding it. Pokey's sunny disposition kept her from brooding about her beginnings, and her older sisters and brother fought anyone who even looked askance at the pale eyed, dark haired child who found joy playing alone with all the toys nature provides for the soul attuned to its beauty. Her dolls were shucks and corn cobs, her horse a crooked stick with vine reins. She loved the smooth pebbles and shiny rocks in the creek. She spent hours drawing in the sand, weaving vines, decorating them with colored leaves, and later her sisters gave her scraps from their sewing and she created small colorful clothing for her crude dolls. She was different, fey, took after her Irish ancestors, they said with a knowing smile.

They had just finished a meager meal of turnip soup, Pa, Mary, Margaret, Eliza and Pokey, when a squawk and clatter began in the barn. Pa made the girls hide in the big wardrobe while he went to see what the Dam Yankees wanted this time. Pa seemed twice his 50 years, with a gimp leg from a fall from the barn loft, his bald head and stooped shoulders portraying the defeat felt by all of Corinth those days. The Yankee camp had drained the town.

His shout was unanswered by the half dozen soldiers already galloping into the dusk. He looked in the barn and then ran to the house to share this glimmer of salvation with his three older daughters and Pokey, his baby. Their own cow, a dozen hens, wooden crates of flour, sugar and coffee, even jars of vegetables and fruits, all left by the Yankees with no explanation. Only Pokey understood. Little sisters are special even if they aren't your little sister.

The war finally ended and Rass was safely home. But he and the older girls soon went their own ways each marrying and moving to their own homes. Rass moved to Jackson to find a job.

Pokey didn't go to school anymore. She had tried for a while, but the teacher decided she had a vision problem. She couldn't see the words on the board, and the letters in the books were jumbled. Of course, she had no problem gazing out the window at the hawks swooping down on their unsuspecting prey. She was sure Pa understood. At night when she nestled close to him as he read from the Bible, he often traced the lines with his finger so she could keep up. But there was just too much excitement and contentment in the fields, the woods and along the creeks to spend the days in a room with so many people.

When the girls married and left Pokey and Pa, they got along fine, Pokey working harder than two men to keep Pa from overwork. But still he was failing fast.

Life had been lonely for the young Pokey. Once a week Billy Jobe, the blacksmith's young brother, would come to help her with the chores. Pa was in bed most of the time now. And once a week Pokey would ride into town to help Billy. He roped wild horses on the prairie and green-broke them to sell to the Army. Billy would not let her ride them, although she could ride as well as he could. But she held them for him to mount, opened gates, and sometimes helped him up when he was thrown.

When he had several horses tame enough, he would drive them to the Fort. Pokey usually rode with him to the river and watched him cross. The next day she would meet him at the river. They planned to marry soon, but Pa wanted them to wait for a while, hating to share his last child.

When she went to meet him the last time, she saw him on the bank of the river. A drifter headed for the fort had gone with

Billy, and obviously robbed and killed him. Everything was gone, his horse, saddle, coat, and hat. She lifted his body on her horse and cried for the second time in her life, for Billy, and for their lost dreams.

The crows cawed in the field where the brown corn stalks still stood. The sound reached Pokey without fully awakening her. Maybe it was the crows, or the draft from the cold grate, or just the loneliness. She was alone. She knew before she opened her eyes and lifted the dear gnarled hand of the man who had been her own special Pa for sixteen years. Last night she had brought him a cup of warm milk and lifted his head while he sipped it. She had pleaded more with her eyes than her soft voice, but Pa wouldn't talk about the night the Indian slept on the hearth. Now she would never know.

Pokey remade the fire, as though it could bring warmth to the cold body lying on the bed. She heated meal mush, ate it, and went to the old wardrobe to get her shawl. Beside it lay the Indian blanket. She held it, burying her face in it and sobbed for the third time in her life. Braiding her long dark hair in one heavy plait, she looped it into a knot on the back of her head. She squared her slim shoulders and got out the high-buttoned shoes she had never worn. She had promised Pa she would be a lady someday, and the day had come. With one last sniff of its pungent folds, she tossed the blanket into the fire and watched the fabric curl and crumble in the flame. Then she wrapped her shawl about her body and walked the mile to sister Mary's house. How do you ask your favorite sister if she is really your sister? Of course, you don't. Maybe Mary didn't know the answer either. If she did, she wasn't telling.

Pa had made them all promise to give the house and land to Pokey. The others were married and Pokey was the baby. Besides her eyes were weak. Oh, Pokey could see. She could see the crows in the blue fall sky, and the sunrise on the corn field. She could see every leaf on the willows along the creek bank, and she could read Pa's Bible. Pa thought she had memorized the passages he read after supper every night, but she could read it all. It gave her a calm feeling to say the words even when she was too young to understand. She didn't read the books at school. If she squinted she could not see them clearly, and why go to school if you can't see. Mary knew her secret and often helped her with difficult words. It was more fun to work with Pa and wade in the creek. But no more. Now Pokey was a lady.

Sparks from the anvil danced like fireflies and the clang made the music as Pokey waited for John Jobe to shoe her horse. She paid him with shuttered eyes, ignoring the stubby fingered grimy hand offering to help her into the side saddle. She had not ridden bareback since Pa died. But one day, her time would come! Life had been frustrating for Pokey since she decided at sixteen to keep her promise to Pa. Her sisters refused to let her live alone. Eliza was first to offer a plan. She, her "sickly" husband and two children would be glad to move in with Pokey. Eliza and Pokey tried hard to make ends meet, but five mouths to feed and only two women to do the farming and the housework, and Tom's demands for whiskey soon took their toll on the two women. Tom found a widow who was willing to put up with his problem just to have a man around the house. Eliza and her children moved in with

Margaret. Several families in succession rented Pokey's house for a stop-over on their way to Texas or California. Pokey, in the meantime, tried to make a success of keeping house for Mary, whose husband was the sheriff. Mary cooked and cleaned the jail, and Pokey kept the garden and cared for her sister's children. They had tried to reverse roles, but even Mary's husband had a roving eye and too many hands when the beautiful Pokey was around.

John Jobe had come calling several times, hoping to get Pokey alone, but thus far she had avoided any discussion. She could not be unkind, John meant well, but a marriage like her sisters' just would not do for Pokey.

A block from the blacksmith stable, she answered the respectful nod of the gentleman with long whiskers. He reminded her of Pa, not as old of course. Mr. Josiah Wood must be at least thirty, and so distinguished. He was new in town, from Georgia he had said at dinner last night. Her brother-in-law had brought him home to discuss renting Pokey's place. Pokey was reluctant to agree to the trade. She just couldn't see her crows, creeks and willows belonging to someone else. There was a substance about Mr. Wood. He would make the farm pay, and want to buy it. Then it would be lost to her forever. On impulse she turned her horse and rode back to the hitching post at the hotel.

"Mr. Wood," she spoke softly, "I would like to ask your advice. Mr. Jobe has asked me to marry him. Would you advise me to accept?" Her heart raced as she saw the twinkle in his eyes. "Why Miss Pokey, I was going to ask you myself!" he drawled.

Pocahontas Taylor Phillips married Albert Josiah Wood six months later. It would have been sooner, except for the meddling visitors from Georgia who told her brother-in-law that he was already married. It took a while to dissolve his unhappy alliance with the woman in Georgia, and to clear up the matter of his hasty departure from Pike County after a family feud. None of these facts bothered Pokey. She felt a security with Hick that no amount of criticism from her family could shake. He laughed at her name for him. Her brother-in-law had unwittingly given it to her. He had bellowed. "Why Pokey, you can't marry that hick from Georgia!" But she did. They moved into her home and Hick proved her confidence in him. He worked eighteen hours a day with Pokey at his side, improving the house, planting a garden, helping neighbors build houses and barns and three prosperous years, two babies and a great deal of happiness later, the Woods traded their property to a family from Texas who had made money on cattle in Palo Pinto County on the Brazos River. They were tired of the hardships and wanted to return to civilization. The deal was made, equipment traded, advice shared, and with all their belongings, the Wood family started out to Texas. The Coles had told Pokey to take everything she needed, there were no resources except the land itself, and it was a hard unrelenting land. Pokey could not leave the blue and white dishes with "England" stamped on the bottom. Pa had told her they were his wedding present to his wife, brought up the Mississippi by boat from New Orleans. Pa had hidden them under the house when the Yankees raided. She wrapped them safely in quilts. Hick packed wisely too. He took seeds, sapling fruit trees, chickens, tools, and one wagon load of pipes and equipment the Coles said would be useful during the droughts. When Pokey asked him if he was going to put the house on a wagon, he laughed.

The wagon train left Corinth among cheers and tears. Pokey's sisters had misgivings, but Pokey was content. She had told Hick when he considered the trade, that she would go to the end of the earth with him, and feel safe doing it. They took three wagons drawn by mules and horses. The Coles' oldest son had begged to stay in Texas, and now pleaded to return with the Woods. He drove the first wagon, with Pokey and the children in the second one. Hick, with his heavy equipment, brought up the rear with the strongest mules. They had a rough map and Will's memory to guide them. They had provisions for dry camp, but occasionally passed small settlements in Mississippi and Louisiana. When they crossed the Red River into Texas, they left all civilization behind. Only the barren range extended before them. The two month trip was physically hard, but the happy group made the most of it. Each night when they stopped, they freed the animals, even the chickens from the coop. Strangely, none of the animals wandered away.

It seemed the totally deserted plains were a threat to them, and they stayed near the wagons. Even the rooster found his way back to his cramped coop after an hour of scratching in the dirt. The children adored Will, who was excited about going home again. For Hick, it was another challenge, an adventure of a lifetime, and for Pokey just another labor of love. Late one afternoon, they came to a wide stream bed with only a trickle of water. Will recognized the spot, and they knew they had reached the Brazos. They camped there, rested the animals and awoke with excitement the next day. Home was only a day's ride south along the river.

Will could not hold back the tears when they found the house he had helped build burned to the ground. The barn was still there, and the friendly Indians who had worked with the Coles were glad to see the white family, which would again improve their lifestyle.

The Indians were drawn to Pokey at once. She loved them all and shared many of their skills. They made blankets very like the one she had burned when Pa died, but they did not like her beads. "Pache!" She put them away, unable to throw them away because the Indian woman had left them for her and they <u>were</u> pretty! Strung on a strong cord made from braided horse tail hairs, they were not clay, like the Navajos made, but actual multicolored stone in different shapes.

The very pregnant Pokey established an easy-going routine preparing simple meals and caring for the children while Hick, Will and the Indians went to work. A house would have to wait until crops were in, trees planted, and a crude irrigation system in operation. The Indians taught Hick to dam up low spots on the prairie to make rain reservoirs, or tanks, to water the cattle. Near each tank and at the home site, Hick sunk pipes deep into the ground to make pumps to use when the river was dry, as it was now. Pokey's third child, a boy, was born in a large wooden box the Indians had covered with brush and lined with hides to make a shelter. The children loved the Indians' homes. They were reluctant to move into their new house when it was finished in the late fall, after crops had been gathered.

Hick had immediately begun building up his herd from strays from the prairie and stock bought from other ranchers who had also given up the hard way of life. Hick and Will ventured far from the ranch, leaving Pokey and the children in the care of the Indians. Pokey later said she had gone five years without seeing a white person except for Will and her own family. Then she remembered the injured stranger. While Hick and Will were gone, she and the children rode horses bareback to the tanks miles out on the prairie to spend the day pumping water into the ponds for the thirsty cattle. One day they found a seriously wounded man. He would have died there, but Pokey bound his bleeding leg with strips from her own clothes. Ella rode back to the Ranch to get the Indians, who came and made a rough sleigh of brush to pull him to the ranch house. He staunchly refused to tell them his name, or how he had been shot. He said it was best to just call him Andrew. When he left Pokey promised to name her expected baby for him, but Andrea was just too much name for the dark-skinned whirlwind little girl, so she became "Annie." She was born with a black birthmark on her upper leg in the same location as Andrew's wound. Another son, Gordon, was born, and two more died at birth and were buried on the prairie. The family was always busy planting the rich soil in the spring, irrigating from the river in season, and the wells in dry weather. In fall they harvested the crops and put up provisions for their winter and for the cattle. Hick planted cotton and it flourished with the water his ingenious system supplied. His trees grew and bore fruit. His herds grew and he and Will drove cattle to Fort Worth to sell. They took their wagons of cotton to Mineral Wells to the gin, selling most of it there, but saving Pokey some for her carding and weaving. The trips kept the men away for weeks, and Pokey and the children were happy with the Indians. Pokey never seemed to worry. She was always well and strong, and taught her children to accept and survive. She often reminded them that the Lord had given them so much, and He wanted them to be happy.

Several times during their fifteen years on the prairie, they faced the devastating phenomenon   the Texans called a "Blue Norther" .. The first time it happened, the men were out doing their late afternoon chores when the Indians ran to them pointing north. The sky was black, resembling smoke from a prairie fire. Will remembered such an experience and they rushed to get the stock in the barn and take wood and water inside. The Indians refused shelter in the house, disappearing in their hogans. The wind was gale force, frozen rain blew parallel to the ground, and the temperature dropped from forty to ten degrees in thirty minutes. They would have been terrified except for Will's assurance that the freeze would only last a few days. It was difficult not to harbor some fear that they had taken on too much, but the next day when they saw the Indians running to the barn to check the stock, they returned to a very cold but normal routine. It was several days before they could check the cattle on the range. Most had survived the cold, probably because they were fat and healthy. The few frozen ones were butchered and eaten or stored.

But Winston, Pokey's second son, who had weak lungs from asthma, was critically ill. Pokey stayed by his side day and night, making a tent of quilts to help him breathe. Near the end, as Pokey held him close, he rasped, "Texas is good. I'm glad Pa brought us here."

A young neighbor from the ranch a hundred miles south of them had been stranded during the storm. He was on his way home from a wedding in Mineral Wells where he had played his fiddle. He stayed a while after the storm subsided to help the sad family. It was almost a week before the frozen ground could be penetrated. Pokey would always keep those sad times in her heart. She said she would never forget the beautiful strains of Scott Moore's fiddle, and the deep bass voice of Will Cole as he sang "There will be an uncloudy day," and the words of her son as he was dying.

A week after the storm their nearest neighbor, who lived more than fifty miles away, came with his wagons loaded and driving his herd of cattle. The storm had defeated him. His wife and one child had died, and many of his cattle had frozen. He wanted to give his cattle to Hick and go back East in defeat. But Hick, good business man that he was, saw a profit in sight. He paid the going rate for the scrawny herd, knowing his water and feed would fatten them fit for market by spring, and sent the neighbor on his trip.

After fifteen very profitable years on the prairie, Hick returned from Fort Worth one day to say they were moving to the small town of Garner, one hundred fifty miles away. He had bought a few acres on the outskirts of town and hired some men to build a house for them. Will and Allie immediately told Hick they were planning to be married, and would like to stay on the ranch. Hick was pleased with the plan. He had hoped the Indians would keep the herd up so he could turn a profit, but with Will there it would be assured. Pokey hated to leave her Indian friends. They had seemed like family to her, but she never questioned Hick's wisdom. The younger girls were ecstatic over the move to town. Ella, the oldest, had a natural talent. She copied a picture in a magazine for Allie's beautiful wedding gown. With all the materials available in Garner, she dressed the girls like princesses. They went from country girls to town society in a few weeks. But not Pokey, she never changed.

Hick continued his prosperous operations, building a gin in Garner so the farmers did not have to take their cotton to Mineral Wells to the nearest gin. The train now came to

Garner, and he extended credit to the farmers until their cotton was sold. Soon he had a farmers and ranchers bank in his home and often bought cotton directly from the farmers who were in need, holding it himself until prices went up. Hick earned a reputation in Garner. On the prairie he had no competition except the elements, and he defeated them soundly. Here in Garner he had the money to make good deals, the confidence to take risks, and the trust of the people who saw him as a shrewd business man, but never dishonest. He never misled his friends, he explained the odds to them, but they were not in financial position to take the risks he did, hence they got by, and he profited. Two times a year Hick took Pokey to see Allie and her children at the ranch. Life in Texas had been good to the Woods.

Two letters brought mixed emotions and a chance for a change. Pokey's sister, Mary, in Corinth, was quite ill. She was Pokey's last living sister and Pokey wanted to see her. It had been eighteen years since they left Mississippi. Hick had agreed to take Pokey on the train to Corinth when he received a letter from his brother in Georgia.

His twenty-five year old feud was settled. The man Hick had seriously wounded had died of natural causes, and none of his family was left to cause problems. Hick could now go home to see his brothers and his aged mother. They decided to combine the trips. Leaving the younger children with their very capable sister Ella, Hick and Pokey went by train to Corinth. There she visited her old home, the graves of her parents and sisters, and spent some time with Mary. The realization that she had only a short time to live loosened Mary's resolve, and she told Pokey all she remembered about Pokey's birth, her Indian mother, and the oath they had all taken never to tell. Pokey felt little surprise and no resentment, just love for the family who had raised her. She explained all this to Hick on their trip on to Georgia. The mystery of her birth had been so important in her youth, but the wonderful years they had together in Texas overshadowed all else. Hick teased her and called her his squaw, but his love and pride were always evident to all who saw the shrewd business man and his gentle happy wife.

The Woods in Pike County, Hick's mother, two brothers and their families loved the still beautiful Pokey, and doted on their long lost younger brother. Inevitably, Hick wanted to move to Georgia, and predictably, Pokey acquiesced.

When Hick and Pokey returned to Garner, they found their youngest daughter, Annie, had eloped while they were away. She would not be going to Georgia with them. Annie and her young husband, Scott would begin their life together on thirty acres, which, along with a mule, had been a wedding gift from his father. Annie was pleased, having spent most of her life on a farm.

Hick sold their home and the gin, and went with Pokey to the ranch to confront Will and Allie. The young couple decided to move to Georgia also. They packed belongings and planned to drive the last of the cattle to market. As they sat on the back steps for the last time, Hick saw tears on Pokey's cheeks. He was afraid he had forced the move on her too fast, but she assured him for the third time in their married life that she would willingly go anywhere with him.

"I am crying for the babies we will leave buried here on the prairie, for Gordon who will stay in Garner, and for my Indian family."

Hick decided then to give the house and remaining stock to the Indians. As they rode away the next day, Pokey laughed.

"I wonder if they will wait until we are out of sight before they burn the house down!" she quipped. Pokey was not one to cherish possessions. A thousand memories were hers to keep, and all she surveyed was hers to enjoy. She left Texas with her two oldest, Ella and Brad. In the pocket of her new black taffeta coat were her Indian beads, more special now to her. She felt they held some meaning of her past which eluded her. And in her lap, wrapped in her favorite quilts, was the last piece of the blue and white ironstone china from England. "Hick has always been a good provider. We will have everything we need."

On the train trip, Pokey told the children about her Indian heritage, and they were horrified. They had loved the Indians on the prairie, but their newly acquired city pride had changed them. They begged Pokey to never tell anyone about her mother. She smilingly agreed; it mattered so little now.

Pokey loved Georgia. It was so like her beloved Mississippi. They bought a farm ten miles from Zebulon where Hick's brothers lived. Neighbors in the small town near them welcomed the family and soon Hick was in business as usual. He built up their farm, irrigated the fields and was as successful here as he had been in Texas. He built a gin and began adding to his already adequate financial resources.

When Annie, who had remained in Texas, wrote that she was expecting her first child, Hick persuaded her to come to Georgia to have her baby. Scott came on the train with her and reluctantly left her to return to Texas. Perhaps he knew then that his marriage was over. Three times he came to get his wife and baby daughter, but each time he found the Wood family bonds too strong to break. So he returned to Texas and sold their land. "Scott started to roam with his fiddle," as his brother told Annie when he wrote her about Scott's death in Utah. When his brother, Ed, went to claim Scott's body and bury him, he found Scott had bought a little gold locket for his daughter and left a note telling Ed to find a picture to put in it so his princess would not forget her father.

Pokey fiercely loved the baby, calling her a poor fatherless child. Perhaps she remembered her wistful childhood in Corinth. Perhaps she sensed that Annie was not really interested in parenthood. Instead she worked outside from dawn till dusk beside her father, happily pursuing the lifestyle she loved in Texas

When he cleared trees to open a new field Annie worked right beside him. One day as they worked, a stick went into Hick's eye and penetrated the eye ball. It blinded him in that one eye, and was very painful. During his convalescence, it was Annie who nursed him and put the bandages on his eye while Pokey looked after the baby and did the outside chores. Ella was ever the capable housekeeper, and Brad, the older son had been elected Sheriff of the county. When Hick recovered, he bought Annie a beautiful gold watch on a chain and had it engraved. "For being my nurse," he said.

After Hick's eye healed, he relied more and more on Annie to conduct the businesses. His employees called her "Hick's Annie" and respected her decisions as they did his. Pokey said

Annie was more like Hick than any other child they had. "Give them a handle and they will run with it!" As Annie filled the place by Hick's side on the farm and in the gin, Pokey took over care of Annie's child. The spoiled child was a handful, determined to upset Hick and seek refuge under Pokey's apron. She let the dogs into the smoke house, locked the cats in the harness house, scattered fresh picked cotton over the muddy yard, rode a horse up and down the rows of corn, destroying two acres of the crop; she led the goat into the garden, and painted the white front door with red poke berries. Pokey reminded Hick that, but for him, the "little Moore youngun would have been raised in Texas!"

Hick was eighty now but continued to work like a young man. When he finished his own work, he volunteered to help his neighbors. One such day he had spent the morning putting shingles on a friend's barn. When he came home for his noonday meal, he stopped outside to chop stove wood. Pokey went to the porch to call him to dinner and watched him raise the ax. Suddenly he stiffened with the ax still in his hand. He was gone when she got to him. Later she said he went just as he would want to go – still a strong man, working his way to heaven, not waiting to be called, but she added that she would have rather lost any child she had than her dear Hick.

After Hick's death, Pokey divided her farms between the children and she and Ella moved into a house next door to the gin. Pokey and Annie continued to operate the gin. Annie married and moved to her new home five miles away so the ten year old "fatherless child" could walk between the two houses and still be with her beloved Pokey.

Ella's talent as a seamstress was well known. She kept their home beautifully appointed for a small town home, and clothed their family and half the town in true fashion. Pokey's lifestyle changed, but Pokey did not. She maintained her indomitable spirit, raising her grandchildren, keeping up her garden, her orchard and her home, visiting and helping neighbors in need, and bringing joy to those she touched. In good weather, she could always be seen sitting on her porch reading her bible without glasses. She never needed them.

Annie's baby had grown up now and married. She and her children visited often, still drawn to the ever-loving Pokey who pieced beautiful quilts from Ella's scraps, many original designs and some copies of ones she had seen in Mississippi and Texas. Every child and grandchild was presented with these treasured works.

Then when Ella died, Pokey insisted on living alone, continuing her simple life style and helping with the business of the gin next door. She visited neighbors and was always welcome. She knew when to take a freshly cleaned chicken and a dozen eggs to tide some family over, and when to just take a basket of fruit or a vase of flowers and good advice for the unhappy ones.

One winter, Georgia had a brutally cold spell. Pokey said it was like a Texas "Blue Norther." She went out to bring wood for her fire and slipped on the ice. Her leg was broken, and while she could crawl up the steps, she could not reach up to open the door. As she lay huddled against the door for warmth, she made her plans. She would spend the winter with Annie.

But that was just a beginning. She would sell the gin and build a church with a cemetery on her land. Her house would serve as a parsonage and she could have Hick and Ella moved from the Wood cemetery. Then she could drive the buggy to see them when she visited her old neighbors.

During the last few years of her life, Pokey spent much time reminiscing about her youth in Mississippi and her years on the prairie in Texas with Hick and the Indians who helped them to survive there.

One great granddaughter especially loved to walk beside the old lady, or sit at her feet and hear her tales. The child seemed to share Pokey's love of the earth, all living things, and God's gift to those attuned to the elements. Once after a long walk, they were sitting on the steps resting. Pokey was now ninety years old, and almost as spry as the twelve year old Martha.

"Child, I've talked to you about my life more than to anyone else ever. I guess it is because I feel you hear more than the words. Maybe someday you will write my story. I know there was beauty and goodness there because I am so content now to wait for God's will. But there is sadness and mystery too that I can't explain. When others were learning to write their feelings, I was on the banks of the creek and in the fields and woods.

Her good night to Annie was a cheerful one.

"I dread the sting of death, but I don't mind dying. I will be with Hick and my babies." True to her nature, Pokey slipped past the sting and went peacefully in her sleep that night.

It was many years later when the child, Martha, was a grandmother herself, that her search for her own grandfather's grave led her to Utah. He had died at age twenty-five in Ogden, Utah after his wife, Annie, and daughter had not returned to Texas with him. The little cemetery was as flat as a table, completely square and well-tended in spite of the age of the monuments.

After her unsuccessful search in Ogden the previous day, someone mentioned the "old" cemetery up in the hills. Now she could just see some of the taller buildings of Ogden nestled in the valley, but the encircling panorama of stark-peaked Rockies took her breath. They dwarfed the domed Blue Ridge Mountains of her home state.

The stone gate house was closed, the sign read:

Open 10 – 4 Monday – Friday

She tried the gate in the old iron fence and finding it unlocked, she stepped in. A narrow dirt roadway divided the square into four sectors. She systematically searched each sector, and was losing hope when she found it in the last square near the back fence. A weathered stone, but legible.

Scott Moore

1879 – 1904

Her crusade to find her grandfather was over. Just twenty five, he hardly knew his five year old daughter, his "princess" and he would never know his grandchildren. She placed the wilted flowers on the monument, and as the tears fell, she murmured, "I'm sorry it took me so long, Grandfather." Standing alone in the still dusk, she thought of another story. Not too many miles over those mountains was Salt Lake City, where she would return her rented car and board her plane. That was also the location of the Mormon Archives and Library. Could she learn anything about a name that was only vague memory from childhood? Several days later a bemused woman boarded her plane for Georgia. She knew in her heart that she had found her great great grandfather, Pokey's father.

Jonathan Taylor, son of one of Joseph Smith's trusted elders, had left the church when he was thirty to live among the Indians in West Texas and New Mexico. He moved from village to village, not preaching or postulating, but teaching and improving the lifestyle of the Navajos. He was said to be searching for his youngest wife, an Indian girl who had disappeared while he was away from the village.

After ten years away, he returned to Salt Lake, an old man despite his mere forty years. He spent the remainder of his life spearheading a movement to abolish polygamy in the Mormon Church, but died before his dream was realized.

The high marbled hallway was bare and cold as a tomb. Gloomy thoughts for a young woman hoping to land a job. The past five years of anguish had robbed her of her sunny smile and perpetually expectant attitude, but not her beauty. Her dark hair was straight and long, her skin smooth and unlined, almost sallow, but saved by her stark black lashes and brows, and a naturally pink mouth.

A happy childhood with loving parents had not prepared her for the realism of a cruel husband and a broken marriage. Ten years of contentedly sharing a life were ended.

Now with two children and small support payments, a full time job with benefits was necessary. Ten years ago she would have faced this new phase of her life with enthusiasm. This drab, listless woman was a stranger even to herself.

The personnel manager had sent her down the hall to the last room on the right. The man in the doorway took a few steps into the hallway and stopped. He was silhouetted against the ivory walls so she could not see his face, or his startled expression. Some instant sense of recognition struck her, and she almost cried out, "It's – " then she lost the image, and walked hesitantly to meet him.

An hour later a bemused girl waited for the elevator. How could she feel so different? How had he charmed her into talking so openly about her youth, her horses, her sons, the dreams she had thought were lost to her, and her love of the west, especially New Mexico, where she had begun her marriage?

The green-eyed balding sorcerer had actually convinced her they wanted her to work with the new computer system. He had said they needed her confidence and enthusiasm.

Two weeks later she again walked down the marble hall. This time no illusions greeted her. She was welcomed by the small office staff who took her in tow and became steadfast friends.

The work was difficult, a new and challenging experience for the intelligent woman who had quit college in her third year to marry her high school sweetheart. Each day at lunch, she sat on the marble wall outside the building reading a book while she ate her apple. Some days the sorcerer would walk by and chat.

Other days she could sense him watching her from the window far above. The modest girl had no idea of the enchanting picture she presented, always simply dressed, unadorned except for her beautiful dark waist length hair blowing in swirls around her shoulders.

For months she basked in the warmth of suspecting she was admired. She knew her work was excellent and her quick wit appreciated. But too long she had suffered from the self-loathing of a rejected woman. So she expected nothing.

Finally came the day she walked into his office with completed work.

With his beautiful wide smile, he began "I wanted to ask you"

"The answer is yes, what is the question?" Her reply shocked and embarrassed her and sent him into howls of laughter. "Actually I was going to ask you where you got those beautiful beads, but will you tell me while we eat dinner tonight?"

At dinner that night he asked her to tell him all about herself. " Well, I may be part Indian. My great great grandmother's name was Pocahontas."

" Now I can tell you my dark secret," he quipped. " I come from a long line of Mormons. My great great grandfather was an elder in the church. He lived in Utah and had four wives. His name was John Taylor."

"Oh, that is interesting. Pocahontas was "Pocahontas Taylor Phillips. Maybe we are related."

" Oh good Lord, I hope not." They laughed too much to eat much that night.

It was dinner the next night, and for weeks to come, moonlight rides, music, talks, walks, all enchanting times of turning back the hands of time. They laughed and teased each other about being teenagers again.

When he asked to see her horses, she was frightened. No one else could ride her horses. They were large, spirited animals she had raised and trained herself. Suppose he couldn't ride, or got hurt. But she couldn't refuse. When he arrived in old jeans and cowboy hat, she relaxed a little. But only when they were riding through the wooded trails after a romping canter across the pasture did she realize she had found her prize. He could hold hands and ride side by side, and steal an occasional kiss without breaking stride. Strangely, the big grey who rejected everyone except his owner accepted the man docilely.

"Why did you name him Jericho?" he asked one day. They were sitting on the mossy bank of a small stream resting from a long ride.

"My world came tumbling down the night he was born" she replied, wanting to add "But you are building it up again."

Was this love? She was afraid to hope for the impossible. Certainly something she had never felt before had a grip on her. He wasn't really handsome. Tall, strong, lanky, graceful. Tanned leathery skin, the most beautiful clear green eyes she had ever seen, and that smile to light the world. They shared so much. A love of the earth, rocks, wild flowers, birds, horses. It was a new experience to feel so close to someone, to think, feel and say the same things.

If they were not together, they talked on the phone till late every night planning the hundreds of things they were going to do, places to go, dreams to share.

For Thanksgiving they would take their children camping. Next summer, they would go to Yosemite by way of New Mexico, Utah, and Colorado. But it was just September and it was hard to get in all they wanted to do , and say and see, especially when he had to be out of town frequently.

When the phone rang one night, she knew who it would be.

"Anna, please fly to Tampa tomorrow, I have to show you the most beautiful white beach with ripples as far as you can see. You know what I am asking, it's forever? And wear your beads so I'll know my princess."